WOLF

Written by Bali Rai

Illustrated by Kinchoi Lam

Collins

CHAPTER 1

She was crouching in the shadows, the first time
I saw her. Right on the woodland's edge. I spotted
her eyes reflecting the moonlight. A silvery head and
powerful shoulders. I should have felt threatened, but
I didn't. She watched me curiously. We gazed at each
other until my friend, Faith, appeared. Then she ran.

The woods sat on the edge of town, growing smaller each year as more houses were built. Mum and I had loved walking the narrow paths and exploring the undergrowth. Splashing around in the shallow brooks, soaking each other. We'd had picnics by the river, with cakes and sandwiches and fresh lemonade. We had sat and read in the shade. Enjoyed the earthy, sweet scent of the trees and plants and flowers. Watched the ducks and squirrels and mice and birds.

Once the houses were built, our woodland began to disappear. Now, most of the paths and clearings were no more. And nor was Mum.

CHAPTER 2

Dad was Friday-evening tired. He dozed on the couch, not really watching TV. He only noticed me when I turned it off.

"Hey, Verity."

I sat beside him and got a hug. He had strong arms, and I loved being cuddled by him.

"Good day?"

"Yeah," I said. "Grandma made lasagne. You want some?"

"No," he replied. "I had a burger after work."

"Lasagne's really good," I told him.

Dad worked long hours. Luckily, my maternal grandmother lived close by. She visited every afternoon, made dinner and watched over me until Dad got back.

"You busy at work?" I asked Dad.

He smiled sleepily.

"Always," he said. "I'm working tomorrow and Sunday too, sadly. We need to lay the foundations for the next phase of houses being built."

"Oh," I replied, shifting on the old, lumpy, threadbare couch Mum had loved. Throwing it out felt wrong. When I sat on it, I felt more connected to her.

"Once this project's over, we'll go away," Dad said. "Just you and me."

"It's OK," I told him. "You have to work."

"Yes, but I'm due holiday," he said. "And you have a break coming up, so – "

"Cool," I replied.

"You sure you're OK?" he added, sniffing my hair like he did when I was little.

"Same stuff," I admitted.

"Yeah. Me too."

"I'm gonna go read," I said.

"OK," he replied. "I'm going to bed. I'll lock up."

I shook my head.

"Just get some sleep," I told him. "I can lock up."

I didn't read for long. I couldn't stop thinking about Mum and the woods and *her*. My brain felt ready to explode. I needed fresh air.

It was late, but I didn't care. I padded downstairs and locked the front door. After putting on my yellow high-top trainers, I left via the kitchen. Dad was so tired, he would never know.

I grabbed a torch from the shed. Its rusty hinges whined and creaked. The air was warm and close, and insects buzzed all around me. Our garden backed onto what remained of the woodlands and I wandered towards it.

A maple tree stump sat at the end of our garden.
My tree stump. I sat down, eyes closed. I'd spent
many hours there, reading or listening to music
on my phone, or thinking. I remembered Mum's
favourite perfume. How she giggled at Dad's
silly jokes. I recalled her arms wrapped around me.
The warmth in her smile. As each day passed,
the memories grew slightly hazier. It was unsurprising,
I guess. Yet, I hated that it was happening.

I sat for a while before I heard the rustling. I opened
my eyes and *she* was there, barely two metres away,
staring at me …

CHAPTER 3

The intelligence and sadness in her eyes meant
I wasn't scared. I should have been. Wolves are
supposed to frighten you. We are taught that they're
wild and aggressive, but she wasn't. She stood
perfectly still, no teeth bared, no hunched shoulders.
She was calm, and much bigger than I thought.

Over a metre long, and almost
as high, she was magnificent.
She had light silver-grey fur
with black streaks, a wide
snout and a black nose.
Her haunches were
solid with muscle,
her black paws wide.
Each of four toes ended
in razor sharp claws.
Her pale blue eyes
were mesmerising.
She cocked her head,
then laid down.
Almost a friendly gesture.

A muesli bar was in the pocket of my hooded top.
I held it up. "Hungry?" I asked.

She didn't respond, only watched me. I unwrapped
the bar and her nostrils twitched.

"See?" I said. "Delicious."

When she stood again, I saw the power of
her hindquarters. I tossed the treat close to her feet.
She sniffed it.

"Go on," I whispered. "No good to me now, is it?"

She sniffed a little more, then backed off.

"No?" I asked.

I wanted to stroke her fur, but I didn't. The sudden
roar of a car engine spooked her, and she vanished
into the undergrowth.

"Don't go," I called out. "It's only a car."

Later, I dreamt I was back in the woods.
In the darkness, the wolf spoke to me. "Do not be afraid," she said. Her voice was oh so familiar, and then I realised why. She had Mum's voice.

"Darkness isn't threatening," she said. "No need to fear it."

Suddenly, we were running. I followed, trusting her knowledge of the undergrowth – the way I once trusted Mum. Sweaty and panting for breath, I was glad when she eventually stopped.

"My home," she told me.

A den, under a fallen tree trunk, covered in branches and overgrown with weeds. Buried deep in the scrub – hard to spot unknowingly. I was fascinated.

"I hide here," she said. "From your kind."

My knowledge of wolves was limited. Did they even have dens?

"Dens protect our young before they join the pack," she said, reading my mind.

A conker-sized grey pebble caught my eye. I collected rocks and stones, so I picked it up and put it in my pocket. I wanted to become a geologist.

"Where are your young?" I asked.

"Gone," she replied.

"But your pack?"

She settled on her hindquarters, her silvery fur gleaming.

"This was once all forest," she told me. "We wolves passed on stories of that time. Then humans began to destroy it. Soon the forest became a wood. Now the wood is endangered."

"The houses," I whispered.

"Where humans prosper, animals cannot," she said. "When houses rise, we are pushed away. My pack have been starved or killed, or died young – "

"But – "

"I am all that remains," she said.

"That's just wrong," I replied.

"The machines growl nearby," she said. I realised she meant the building work. "Soon they will destroy my last refuge."

"Where will you go?" I asked.

"Go?" she said. "There is nowhere. Besides, I am too old to run."

"But – "

"I will die here," she said. "One way or another."

CHAPTER 4

I woke up hot and tired and dazed. Sunlight streamed
through the window. I wanted more darkness.
My head under the covers, I tried for more sleep.
It didn't work. Growling, I went to clean my teeth.
As I brushed, little flashes of my dream reappeared.
Soon I had recalled every single word, and my
heart sank.

Back in my room, my hooded top lay on
the floor. When I picked it up, the pebble from my
dream fell out. I gasped. Had I really been out in
the woods again? I examined the pebble closely. It was
the same one.

"No," I whispered.

Downstairs, Dad was finishing his breakfast. When I appeared, his bright smile became a frown.

"Hey, kid," he said. "What's wrong?"

I sat and placed the pebble on the table.

"Been collecting again?" he said.

"Yeah, sort of," I told him.

"You look tired."

"I am," I replied.

I felt odd, as though I was still dreaming, perhaps. Cut off from my surroundings.

"You know the woods?"

"What about them?"

"Does it bother you that they're disappearing?"

"Not really considered it," he said. "My company builds the new houses. We don't actually clear the trees."

"But those were *our* woods," I said.

He looked sad for a moment. The golden-brown skin around his mouth creased, and his dark eyes glazed. "Things change," he said. "I can't do anything about the woods."

"But it's wrong," I said.

"It's how things happen sometimes," he said.

He didn't mean to be dismissive, but I felt suddenly irritated.

"So you don't care?" I snapped. "Mum and I loved those woods! And now she's gone and there's nothing left of her!"

"Oh, Verity," he said, "I didn't mean it that way. Of course, I care."

"Doesn't sound like it!"

"Your mum will always be with us," he replied. "In our hearts. She's a part of you. That won't change if the trees disappear."

"Yes, it will!" I yelled. "Of course, it will! That's why I spend so much time there – because I miss her!"

"I miss her too," he told me.

I didn't mean what came next. I wasn't cruel. I loved Dad. I was so angry though. So, so angry.

"You can save the woods!" I insisted.

"No, I can't," he replied. "The decision was made by other people. It's not my fault. I have to do my job – "

"You won't save the woods," I cut him off.

"Verity – "

"And you didn't save Mum either!"

Dad was shocked. His mouth sat open and his eyes grew moister. He stood and put his plate in the dishwasher. "I'll be back around 6 o'clock," he said softly. "Your grandma will be here any second."

He left without another word, passing Grandma as she entered the hallway.

CHAPTER 5

I was miserable all morning. Full of guilt. I cleaned the bathroom and tidied my room. Chores usually stopped me from getting too gloomy. Only I couldn't stop thinking about the wolf.

Later, Grandma called me down for lunch. "I've made sandwiches," she said. "Tuna mayonnaise and cucumber."

"I'm not hungry," I said.

"Nonsense, Verity," she replied.

She was short and thin, with spindly legs and sharp features. Her blonde hair was in a ponytail and she wore grey gym leggings, a yellow T-shirt and brilliant white trainers.

"Are you OK?" Grandma asked. "Your dad said you seemed more unsettled than usual. You've hardly said a word to me."

"It's the woods. I just want to save them."

"Too late," she told me. "And upsetting your dad won't help. He's a brilliant son-in-law and was an amazing husband to your mum before – "

Silence swallowed the rest of her sentence.

"Lunch then," she eventually said.

We ate and then I sat trying to read a book. I wanted to see the wolf again. The pebble was a sign that my dream might actually have been real – as ridiculous as that seemed.

Grandma was wrong about saving the woods. You see, I already had a plan. Seeing the wolf had just made me more determined …

I couldn't focus on my book, so I called Faith.

"Are you still up for the plan?" I asked my best friend.

"Yeah," said Faith. "I'm just a bit scared. I told Marlon. He wants to come too."

Like Faith, Marlon was an old friend from school, but since Mum, I hadn't talked to him much.

"Why Marlon?" I asked.

"Because he cares, like us," said Faith. "And it'll be safer with three of us. Besides, he has his ice hockey stick."

She was right about safety, so I agreed.

"Are you OK, Verity?" said Faith. "The other night you looked spooked."

I decided not to tell her about the wolf. Not yet.

"Don't worry," I replied. "I'm cool."

That afternoon I watched videos online, including some about wolves being endangered. They'd always been feared and hunted by humans. Wolves *were* predators, but that was just their nature. Now, their natural habitats were being destroyed. I was only 13, but even I understood. Animals had as much right to exist as humans did. I wanted to do something to help. Even if it got me into trouble.

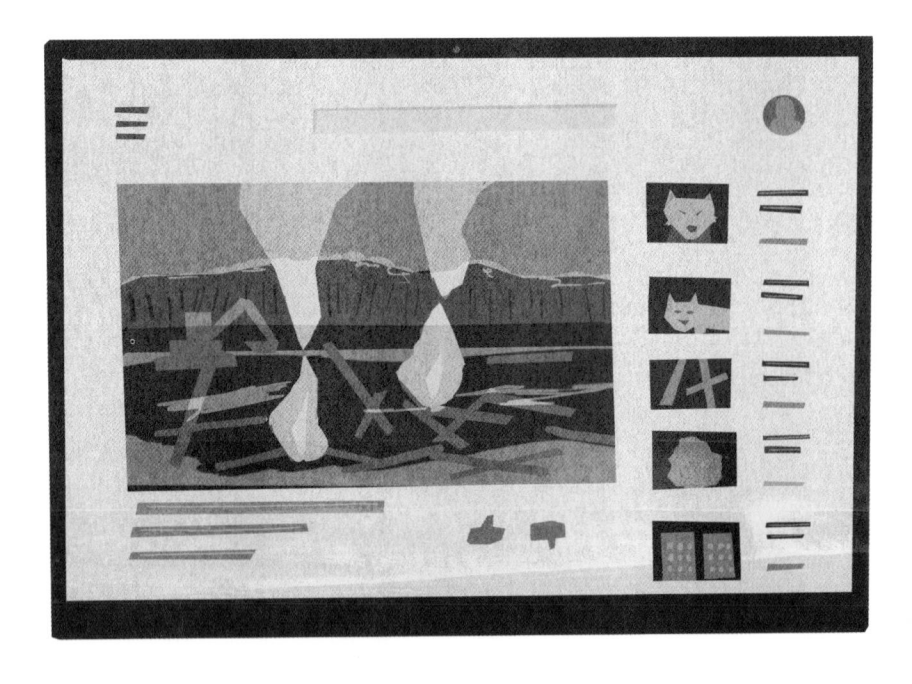

Only, I was torn between doing what felt right, and being sensible. Eventually, I decided to follow my heart. Mum and Dad had always advised me to.

That evening I packed my rucksack with hand sanitiser, some snacks, two bottles of water and something I'd need for my plan. It wasn't much, but it felt like enough. I wasn't going for long. At least, that's what I told myself.

But I *was* going.

CHAPTER 6

I'd set my alarm for 6:30 in the morning. I messaged Dad and Grandma before I left the house. They would guess where I'd gone soon enough. I hadn't exactly kept my thoughts a secret. I didn't want to hurt them. Just make them understand that I was serious.
This wasn't about me. It was about the woods and the wolf, and Mum.

At the end of our garden, I passed my maple tree stump and entered the woodlands. The sky was pinky-blue in the dawn, but to the west, steely grey clouds were moving in, threatening a storm.

I pulled up my hood and crossed the first brook, into the woods. A squirrel darted away, and I heard bird calls and buzzing insects. The dense vegetation and tall trees cast deep shadows. Gloomy days had scared me when I was younger, but Mum had always been reassuring.

"You can't have sunshine every day," she'd say. "And there's beauty to be found in all weather, Verity."

We'd walked most weekends, regardless. I smiled at precious memories of dancing in the puddles as thick raindrops exploded against our faces.

"When you see light reflected through a single raindrop," Mum once said, "like a tear hanging from a petal or branch, you see the power and beauty of nature. Never stop looking, Verity. These woods change every day."

Our woods were all but gone now. Soon, they would be no more. My determination grew and I marched on towards our meeting place. When the first pellet of rain caught my cheek, I didn't care. I was too busy staring at *her* …

She came from a thicket, her wide snout and black nostrils first. Her silvery fur stood out in the low light. She padded towards me, recognition in her beautiful eyes.

"I came to find you," I said. "I know you can't really speak, but – "

"You are wrong."

Her voice rang in my head, impossible yet clear, and Mum's once again. My mouth fell open.

"But – "

"Do you hear me?" she asked.

"Yes."

"Then why do you doubt me?" she asked. "The truth of my voice *is* my voice."

I considered her words. I tried to make sense of the situation, but I couldn't.

"Come with me," she added. "The storm will be heavy."

She cut back through the undergrowth, and
I followed. She was careful to choose a route I could
follow too. Yet I still had to crouch or kneel to
continue sometimes. My face and hands got scratched,
and my jeans and trainers muddy, but I didn't care.
We worked our way north until we emerged by
her den.

"We will shelter," she said.

I watched her jaw as she spoke, but it didn't move.
Yet again, I was confused and amazed, and
a little excited.

I crawled until the space grew wide enough for me to sit. She came after me, and settled on her haunches, eyes fixed to mine.

"Why are you here?" she asked.

"To help protect the woods," I told her. "To save you. My friends are coming, too."

The wolf settled onto her paws. She said nothing for a while. When she finally spoke, she seemed distracted.

"I played here as a pup," she said. "Right by this den. There were still a few of us then. We frolicked in the shallow edges of the river." She closed her eyes.

"We played in the undergrowth, me and my friends. The pack had grown weaker, but we were still a pack – "

"Until the houses were built?"

"Yes," she replied. "And before too. I have my memories, but these are also the recollections of my ancestors. Passed down in a way I do not understand. Sometimes, I remember a past I could never have lived. Images of these lands long before humans came. Nothing but forests and grasslands, stretching away into the distance."

I nodded. "My mum showed me an old map once," I told her. "From about 200 years ago. There was

a small city, but everything else was wild, as you said. It must have been so beautiful."

"It was," she replied. "Or so the memories of my ancestors show me."

"We humans have messed it all up."

"I cannot disagree," she told me. "Your kind do not care for the rest of us. As though this world is yours alone."

"We're not all like that," I protested.

She opened her eyes and stared at me. "No," she said. "You are not."

CHAPTER 7

The storm was heavier than I expected. The rain
pounded like a hundred small hammers against
the den's roof. Thunder rumbled and boomed and,
although I could not see it, lightning crackled
and buzzed. The scent of wet soil and leaves and bark
carried into the den – musty and earthy and metallic.
I loved these sounds and smells, and I felt secure with
the wolf by my side.

"I love the rain," I said.

"I sensed that," she said. "When the last thunder
roll sounded, you smiled."

"Mum and I used to walk in the rain," I replied.
"Dance about and jump in puddles. I was the only kid
I knew who loved thunderstorms."

"What happened to your mother?" the wolf asked.

"She got sick," I replied. "She didn't get better."

"My heart hurts for you," she said.

I watched rain dripping from the den's entrance. A large spider crawled across the dirt, before disappearing under wet leaves.

"You sound like her," I admitted. "Your voice is like Mum's in my mind."

The wolf gazed into my eyes. "I can only hear my own voice. Does it comfort you that you can hear your mother?"

"Yeah," I said. "Feels odd but I like it."

"Odd is sometimes good," she said. It was something Mum had often told me.

"This is all odd," I told her. "I'm not even sure it's real."

"I agree," she said, as another clap of thunder boomed above. "Although that sounds very real."

Eventually, the thunder and lightning passed, and then the rain. It was lighter as we emerged from the den, but the woods were blanketed in shadow. Leaves dripped with rainwater and the ground was boggy in places.

"How close are the machines?" I asked. I needed to get to our meeting place.

The wolf sighed. "Follow me," she said.

This time, she followed a well-worn path, one that I knew. It split in two, one fork towards the river and the other eastwards. Ten minutes after setting off, we reached a chain-link fence. It was three metres high and impossible to get through. On the other side, the woods had been flattened. Earth was piled up, waiting to be reused elsewhere. The giant, bright orange diggers and dump trucks and bulldozers sitting there resembled monsters. Creatures of death and destruction.

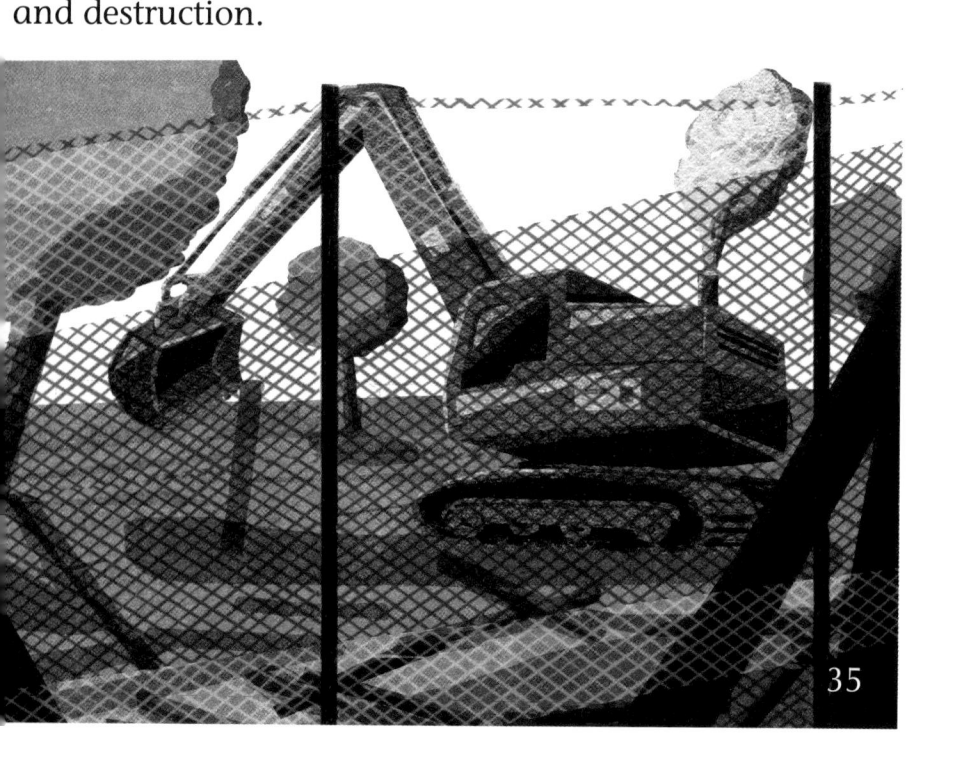

Furthest from us, building works had already begun. Rows of foundations had been dug, and some scaffolding was there too. Two flags sat atop white poles, bearing the crests of the clearing and building companies. One of the logos matched those on Dad's work jacket and polo shirts. I felt a bit sick, and even worse when I thought of Dad and Grandma realising I'd gone.

"There are humans approaching," said the wolf.

"My friends," I explained. "They won't harm you."

But the wolf did not care. She vanished into the undergrowth, as Faith and Marlon appeared.

"Hey, you two," I said. "Ready?"

Faith wore blue jeans, brown boots and a red rain jacket. Her backpack was red too.

"Were you talking to someone?" she asked.

"No," I said.

"I swear we could hear you talking," said Marlon.

He wore black jeans and chunky white trainers, with a grey hoodie and a beanie hat over his cornrows. He had his ice hockey stick with him too, hanging from his rucksack.

"Well, maybe you heard my phone?" I lied. I held it up for them both to see.

"Shall we get started?" said Faith.

CHAPTER 8

Using my phone, I recorded a video of the building site, the fence and the woods behind us. I was careful not to show any of our faces. We took turns to speak. When it was mine, I spoke slowly and clearly, and ended with a plea for help …

"Someone has to stop this madness. We only have one world. We have only one chance. We must start with our own towns and cities. Otherwise, it'll all be too late. Please, please, please watch this video and let's start to save our planet. If we kids can show the adults we mean business, things will change – "

We sent the video to our friends and to a journalist who was a friend of Marlon's parents.

The sudden buzzing of helicopter blades surprised us.

"They're probably looking for us," I said. I quickly turned off my phone in case they could use it to track us.

"Already?" asked Faith. "But that's not possible."

"That's just a regular patrol," said Marlon. "They fly over the site most weekends."

"We should still hide," I said. "They might spot us."

The woods were sodden and the ground muddy. The air was thick and the temperature had risen again. As we hid in the undergrowth, I could feel my scalp begin to sweat. I wondered if the wolf was close by, watching us all.

Her voice appeared in my head. "Your kind believe they are superior," she told me. "They are arrogant enough to think they can control nature. But the thunder will roll, and the lightning will strike long after they are gone. The rivers will rise and fall, and the seeds will become weeds and grow into plants and flowers and shrubs and trees."

"Mum taught me that humans are a part of nature," I said to her in my head. Faith and Marlon would think I'd lost my mind if I spoke out loud. "We aren't separate from it, or special compared to the rest. That's why I want to stop this. We have to start somewhere."

"So, this is about your mother, too?" said the wolf, and I wondered how she knew.

I imagined her on her haunches, graceful and beautiful and powerful.

"I couldn't help Mum," I replied. "I couldn't save her."

"So, saving the woods, saving me, is a chance to make amends?" said the wolf.

"It's more than that," I said. "It's about believing that things can be better."

"Hope, then," said the wolf, making my thoughts clearer for me.

"Hope," I agreed.

CHAPTER 9

We needed to find cover from the storm while
we waited. Marlon led the way, pushing through
the thick vegetation with his hockey stick, with Faith
and me behind him. It was hard going, but eventually
we found shelter under a tree, close to where the wolf
had made her den.

"This should be fine," said Marlon.

"Who died and made you the leader?" said Faith.

He grinned. "You know I'm right!"

I remembered how close we had once been.

He looked at me and shrugged.

"I was sorry to hear about your mum," he said. "She was a good lady."

"That's OK," I said. "I kinda lost touch with everyone but I'm getting better."

"Remember the skateboard?" he said, with a grin.

We had been seven years old, and Marlon got an awesome skateboard for Christmas. The snow had been deep that year, but we decided to take it around the block anyway.

"You crashed right into Mr Reynolds' SUV!" he said.

"Not funny!" I replied. "I banged my head – "

"Old man Reynolds was going crazy!" said Marlon. "And your dad, too!"

"Cost 500 dollars to fix the mess," I reminded him. "And I got grounded for a month."

"You and me both," said Marlon.

Faith looked at me and smiled. "You two were always messing up," she said.

"Her fault," said Marlon. "I was a Grade A student until she came along."

"More like Grade Z," I told him.

We talked for ages about our memories and ate our snacks. I felt happier than I had in a very long time. Normal, almost.

"Should we try and rest?" asked Faith. "I hardly had any sleep. I was too worried my alarm wouldn't go off."

"Guess so," said Marlon. "It might be a long day ahead."

"We should be safe here," I added. "And we won't know how well our video worked for a few hours yet."

"We still going with the second part of the plan?" asked Marlon.

"Why?" Faith replied. "You chicken?"

"Course not!" said Marlon.

"I'll set the alarm on my phone," said Faith. "Two hours?"

Marlon and I nodded.

The ground was damp but OK and covered with twigs and leaves. We settled back, using our backpacks as pillows. I finished my chocolate bar and lay down to rest. Faith and Marlon were soon dozing, so I turned and stared out at the woods.

She appeared about ten metres away, fur glistening in the rain.

"Don't be afraid," I heard her say. "I will watch over you."

* * *

I awoke with a shiver, my legs stiff. The wolf was lying beside me, eyes wide open.

"What time is it?" I asked.

"I don't understand," she said.

"Like, what time in the morning."

"I have no need for human concepts of time," she replied. "The sun is rising. The machines will begin growling soon. I must leave now."

As she darted away, I reached for my bag and took out my phone. I turned it on to check the time, and it began to buzz with messages. One after another, on and on, like an avalanche.

"No way!" I said, sitting up.

Faith and Marlon awoke too.

"What's going on?" asked Faith, rubbing her eyes. Marlon stretched and yawned.

Everyone had gone nuts about our video.

"Show me, show me!" Faith squealed.

The three of us crowded around my phone as I flicked through the messages.

"Wow!" I shrieked. "We're really doing this!"

My phone buzzed again. It was a message from the journalist. She was coming to interview us with her crew!

"Maybe we'll be on TV!" said Marlon.

"You might want to sort your hair out," said Faith.

Marlon nudged her. "You can talk!"

"This is way bigger than we thought," I said. "Like, this could go national."

"International," said Faith.

"They have to stop the destruction now," Marlon added.

It was time for the next part of the plan. Inside my bag, I took out an old chain and a chunky padlock. "People like us get called tree huggers, so, let's go hug us a tree."

CHAPTER 10

A sugar maple tree stood close to the construction site. It was old and tall and beautiful, and we'd chosen it for our plan.

I held up the chain and padlock. In the distance, I could already hear a couple of the machines being fired up.

"They'll have to cut this tree down," I said. "Or get around it, to clear the rest. If we're chained to it, they can't cut it down – "

"But they will just cut us free," said Faith. She and Marlon both looked away. They were frightened, and I couldn't blame them. The chains had been my idea, and I had butterflies in my stomach. I couldn't make them take part. That wouldn't be fair.

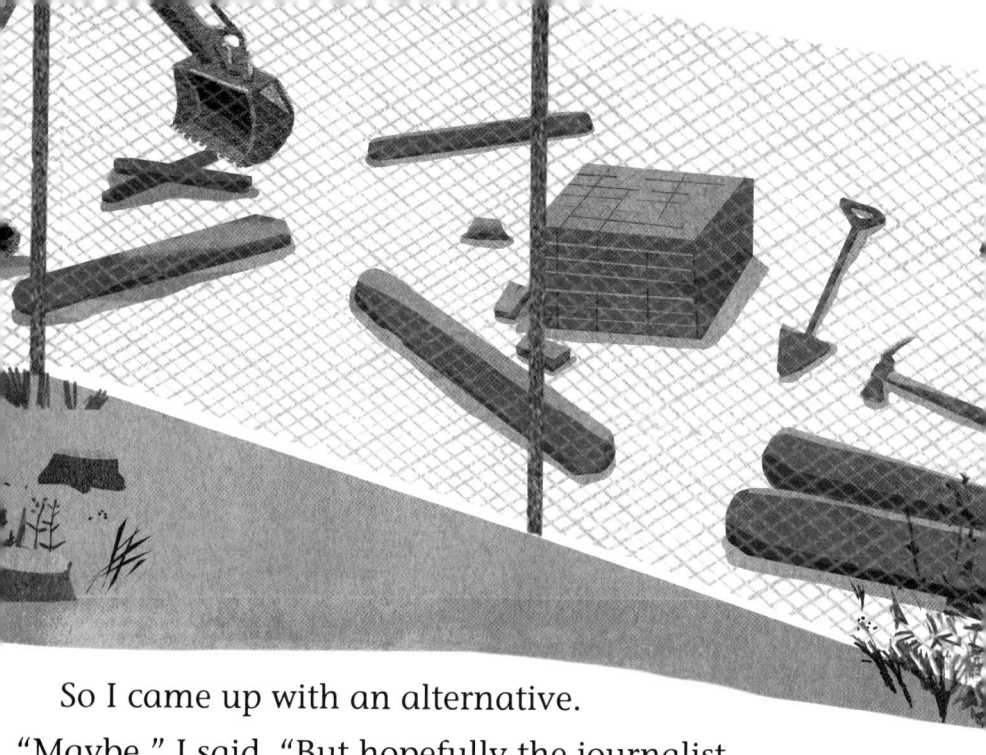

So I came up with an alternative.

"Maybe," I said. "But hopefully the journalist will arrive first. Maybe some of our friends and neighbours too. You'll need to go and round them up."

"I don't understand," said Marlon.

"If we get a crowd, and the media arrive, it might be easier," I replied. "They won't just cut me free. Everything they do and say will be on camera – "

"Just you?" asked Faith.

"Yeah," I told her. "I think you two should get everyone here, if you can. Make some noise."

I smiled, as Marlon and Faith nodded.

I looped the chain around the tree
a few times, and then ducked
under it. Passing the padlock through
several links, I pulled it tight. Then I clicked
the mechanism shut. It was snug but not
too uncomfortable. My arms remained free.

"Loads of our school friends want to
join in," said Faith, showing me the messages
on her phone. "And their parents.
This is awesome!"

It was a great start, but the media had
to arrive before my dad and his workmates.
Otherwise, my plan would be ruined.

"Shall we do another video?" asked Faith.
"Like, if I film you as you're tied to the tree?
I'll make sure they can't see your face – "

"Good idea," said Marlon. "And then we'll go
and round up a posse!"

"Cool."

Faith positioned the camera so that my face
wasn't visible and then said, "Go!"

"*Thank you for watching our video, each and every one of you. I'm now chained to a tree, on site. We will not be beaten. There are animals here that need our protection. There's a wolf – the last of her pack. She's frightened and has nowhere to run. We can't let her die. We just can't. If you can, please come and help. We are not in charge of nature. We are part of nature. Without nature, we are nothing.*"

"Wolf?" asked Marlon, when I was done.
"There aren't any wolves left around here – "

"Trust me," I told him. "Just go and gather
a crowd and I'll explain afterwards."

"You sure you'll be OK?" said Faith.

"Yeah," I said. "I'll be fine."

The grey pebble was in my pocket.
I held it for comfort and courage as my
friends left. I was part excited and happy, and
part anxious. And I still had to face Dad and
his workmates.

They arrived about 90 minutes later.
A van arrived first, one from the site
clearance company. Then another van, and
finally a car, with Dad inside. He wore his work
clothes and heavy brown boots. When he saw
me, he came running.

"Verity!" he cried. "You're OK!"

He looked worn out, upset and happy all
at the same time. I thought he might shout at
me, but he didn't. He just leant in and kissed
my cheek and then held my hand. "I should
have known," he said.

"I'm not going to stop," I told him, pulling my hand away. "I don't care if you're angry with me."

He sighed."I'm not angry," he replied. "I was worried sick and now I'm just relieved. But you have to stop, otherwise you'll be cut free."

"No!" I shouted. "Not until you agree to save the woods!"

His eyes filled with sadness. He looked around at his workmates. They stood a few metres back, whispering to each other. Some of them shuffled with embarrassment.

"We can't save them," he told me. "It's just not possible, Verity."

"But there are animals here," I replied. "There's a wolf. She's the last of her pack and she'll die if you don't stop."

"There are no wolves left around here," he said. "Haven't been any for years. Have you *actually* seen one?"

I nodded. I wanted to say I'd spoken to her, but didn't. That was my secret, and I was keeping it. Besides, Dad and the others would think I'd lost my mind.

"I *have* seen her," I said again. "She's scared and alone. We need to save her."

"But it's a wolf," he replied. "They can be dangerous – "

"Look around, Dad!" I yelled. "It's not the animals destroying the woods. It's humans. We're more dangerous than they could ever be!"

He seemed shamed by my words. He looked away. "I can't change that," he said. "I can't stop this project."

"But – "

"Jas!" a man shouted at my dad. "A word, please?"

The newcomer wore a grey suit, shirt and tie, and a yellow hard hat. He looked ridiculous, but important too.

"That's my boss," said Dad. "Hang on – "

"I'm not going anywhere," I said, half-smiling.

Dad chatted with his boss, who looked sympathetic. He kept glancing over at me. Finally, he nodded and patted Dad on the shoulder. Dad looked annoyed as he trudged back. "He's given me an hour," said Dad.

"What for?"

"To convince you to stop," Dad replied. "It's not his fault, or mine. We don't control what happens to the woods, Verity. We're not bad people."

"What happens if I don't stop?"

Dad grimaced. "Then I guess they will cut you free," he replied.

CHAPTER 11

Faith and Marlon returned 30 minutes later.
I thought they might bring a handful of people
with them. I was wrong. They were leading a crowd of
a hundred or more kids, teenagers and adults – school
friends, neighbours, people I'd never seen before.
It was astonishing. They gathered at a distance and
some of them began videoing the scene.

Verity and Marlon walked up to me.

"Wow!" I said. "You two did good!"

"It was easy," said Marlon. "Everyone wanted
to help. They're all with us."

"My mum is coming too," said Faith. "This is going
to be epic!"

Then Grandma arrived in her running outfit.
"I should be so angry with you!" she said. "But I'm just
glad you're safe."

"I'm sorry," I told her.

"Don't be," she said, surprising me. "You're taking
a stand and I can't be angry. It's a very brave thing
to do."

"Is that the newspaper crew?" I said, as a white van pulled up near the construction gang.

Faith turned and saw them. They had a handheld camera and microphone.

The reporter strode towards us, full of smiles. "Hi, Verity," she said. "I'm Louisa Rawls. You messaged me earlier – "

Dad moved between us. "No," he said. "Verity doesn't want to talk to you."

"I do!" I insisted. "Faith and Marlon, too. Please, Dad – this will help our cause."

Dad glanced at his workmates and then back to me. "You're sure?" he asked.

I nodded.

"OK," said Louisa. "We'll just set up and then get to it. You're causing quite a sensation."

Her grin was wide and warm, and I returned it. "Won't be a moment," she added.

The interview lasted five minutes. Louisa asked what we were doing and why. I told her about the woods and the wolf, and Mum's love of nature, and Faith and Marlon spoke to her too. As soon as we'd finished, Louisa said goodbye and left. It was kind of fun, but I was getting worried about the wolf. Was she still around? Had my actions caused her more grief? I scanned the woods for a sign of her, but she wasn't there.

"Where are you?" I whispered.

"They're calling you Wolf Girl on the news site," said Faith. She held up her phone to show me.

I smiled. "It's not just about me," I replied. "It's you and Marlon, too."

"That's cool," said Marlon. "Every band needs a lead singer. Just glad to be helping out."

I was delighted by the reaction. How could they destroy the woods now? Surely they had to stop?

"My boss called the security guards," said Dad. "Look – "

An SUV pulled up and two uniformed guards got out. They looked uneasy once they saw the crowds.

"I don't care," I replied.

I thought Dad would get angry. I thought he might shout or cut me free himself. He didn't do any of that. He grinned.

"You know what, kid?" he said. "You're right. Hang on – "

He ran to a huge silver SUV with massive tyres. Opening the boot, he searched for something. He came back, carefully avoiding the security guards. I saw what he was holding. It was a length of chain and a padlock.

"Dad?" I said.

"Room for another one?" he said, quickly attaching himself to the tree.

"You don't have to – "

He grinned again. "Yeah," he said. "Yeah, I do."

"You'll get sacked!"

"Probably," he said. "But Harriet wouldn't have let you stand alone. I won't either."

I thought my heart might burst with love. Grandma and Marlon began to laugh, as Faith started filming us again.

"Look at you two," said Grandma. "What a pair of rebels!"

Moments after Dad had joined my protest, the security guards approached us. They ignored me and spoke to Dad.

"Sir, I must ask you to unchain yourself immediately," said the female one.

"I can't," Dad told her. "I haven't got the key. Sorry – "

The guard sighed.

"Well, in that case we'll call the Fire Service and you'll be cut free. Do you really want to put your daughter through that?"

"I can speak for myself!" I yelled. "We will not be moved. Not by you or anyone else!"

"WE WILL NOT BE MOVED!" Faith and Marlon yelled too. "SAVE OUR WOODS! SAVE OUR WOODS!"

The crowd cheered when they heard my words.

I grinned at the security guards. "Everyone is on our side," I told them. "On the side of nature."

The guards started mumbling to each other and trudged away. Some more journalists arrived, alongside more bystanders.

Soon, most of the crowd were chanting: "*SAVE OUR WOODS! SAVE OUR WOODS!*"

"Just wow!" said Faith.

"Double wow," said Marlon.

"Think you've started something, kids," said Dad. He grinned like a child who'd found a secret stash of sweets.

CHAPTER 12

A battered grey jeep turned up before the Fire
Service did. It was covered in dried mud and had
rust patches. The driver's door creaked open and
a man stepped out. He was short, with grey dreadlocks
and skin the colour of salted caramel. His T-shirt read
"Dub Conservation", and he wore khaki combat
trousers and grey work boots. He looked over at me
and raised his hand. I waved back, just to be polite,
and he came over.

"Hey," he said to us.

"Hey," I replied.

"My name is Randall Mortimer," he told us. "I saw
your story online this morning. You mentioned
a wolf?"

Faith, Marlon, Dad and I looked at each other in surprise.

"Yeah," I told the man. "Why, what's it to you, Mr – ?"

"Randall, please," he said, smiling.

"Randall," Dad replied, "why are you asking about a wolf?"

"I'm working with a nature reserve," he revealed. "About 300 kilometres north of here. When I saw the story this morning, I jumped into my jeep and came right down."

I gave him a huge smile.

"Anyway," he continued, "the reserve is a wild animal haven – many that we've rescued from similar developments. We have two other wolves – "

"Wow!" I said. "That's cool, but we want to stop the development."

"Yeah," said Marlon. "We ain't moving until we get what we want!"

"What he said," Faith added.

Randall shrugged. "Not gonna lie, kids," he told us. "It'll be hard to stop. There's too much money involved."

"But I want to save her!" I blurted. "The wolf, I mean."

"You can," said Randall. "I'll take her to the reserve. She'll be safe."

"Take her?"

Randall nodded. "We've got a Government permit to protect and save endangered wildlife. If there's a wolf here, I can stop the destruction for seven days."

I looked at the others. "What do you think?" I asked.

"Randall is right," said Dad. "We might struggle to stop the project. We *can* save the wolf and other animals though."

"Maybe we take that win for now?" said Marlon.

"But you'll get fired, Dad," I replied.

"There's always other jobs," said Dad. "At least you kids stood up for something. That's enough. We can keep fighting, knowing that the wolf is safe."

"I use a very mild tranquilliser," Randall added. "She won't be harmed. It's just to get her back to the reserve. A vet will check her over and then we'll set her free."

I considered what they were saying. It made sense. Even if we did stop the housing development, it would be a long battle. The wolf would still be stuck here, frightened and hidden away. She'd be safer on a reserve.

"OK," I said. "Let's save her and the other animals."

"You're sure?" asked Faith. "I mean, absolutely?"

"Yes," I said. "But do you and Marlon agree, too?"

My friends nodded.

"Cool," I said to Randall. "But you won't need a tranquilliser. Trust me."

Randall told the journalists what we'd agreed. They reacted like crows squabbling over the same meal.

"Verity! Verity!" they shouted. "What do you feel you've achieved? How will you coax the wolf out?"

I could have told the truth, but they would have laughed at me. Instead, I said nothing.

"Where are the keys for the lock?" asked Randall.

"My backpack, over there," I said.

Randall unchained me, and then Dad too. His keys were in his work trouser pocket. When Dad's boss saw us, he started barking orders to his crew.

Randall smiled. "Someone's about to get a shock when I tell him about the permit," he joked. "Leave him to me."

"I'll come with you," Dad told me. "To look for the wolf."

I shook my head. "She won't come out unless I go alone," I told him. "You could keep the reporters away?"

"OK," he said.

He didn't look convinced, but he still backed me. It made me very happy.

"Won't be long," I said.

CHAPTER 13

She was waiting close to the den. Hidden deep in the undergrowth.

"You didn't continue," she said calmly, her icy blue eyes fixed on me.

"A man came to see me," I told her.

"What does this man say?"

"He works on a nature reserve, far from here," I said. "He wants to take you there, so you'll be free and safe."

"Why would he do that?" she asked.

"Because he's like me," I repeated. "He cares about saving nature."

"Do you trust this man?"

"Yes," I replied. "But he needs you to be calm. So that he can take you away safely. Will you let him?"

She edged closer to me and nuzzled my hand. "Tell me what I should do," she said. "I trust you."

When she appeared behind me, everyone gasped. The media crews started reporting live to camera, jostling each other to get the best shot. Randall had his tranquilliser gun on standby. He needn't have. She was calm and obedient. Almost pet-like. Only, she wasn't anyone's pet. She was wild and free, and powerful and huge. Majestic and beautiful. Now, she would be safe too. I was nervous and happy, and a little sad too. I wondered whether I would ever see her again. She licked my hand then, and spoke.

"Perhaps you can visit me?" she said. "Before age takes me forever?"

"I will," I whispered, hoping that it would be possible.

"I'm sure it will be possible," she said.

"Do you hear my thoughts?" I asked.

"Yes," she replied. "I'm not sure why, but we connect somehow."

"So, this is all real?"

I heard her laughter echoing in my head.

"Look at the other humans," she suggested. "Do they think it's real?"

"I meant us talking to each other," I explained.

"Do you hear me?" she asked, as she had when we first met.

"Yes."

"Then, why question it?" she said. "Cherish it, human. I will."

I led her to Randall and my friends.

"She's utterly beautiful," he said, gazing at the wolf. "I can't believe she was here all this time."

"So, so amazing," said Faith.

"Take special care of her," I said to Randall.

"She's my friend."

"I promise, Verity," he said. "Come and see us any time. Your dad has my phone number. Maybe you kids could help out at the reserve. If you *want* to."

Marlon and Faith nodded. I did too.

"We do," I told him.

"YEAH!" said Marlon. "That would be awesome."

Randall opened the rear hatch of his jeep.

"Can you all give us a moment?" I said.

"Sure," replied Randall. "Take all the time you want."

"Us too?" asked Faith.

"Please," I replied. "Just for a minute."

"Cool," said Marlon.

They went over to Dad and Grandma. All around us, everyone watched. But, right then, *she* was the only thing that mattered …

"Your name is Verity," she said.

"Yeah," I whispered.

"Then, goodbye, Verity," she said. "And thank you."

"I don't want you to go," I told her. "I know you have to, but – "

"Sometimes you have to let go," she replied. "For your own good, and for those who leave. But trust in hope. You have given that to me. Take some for yourself, too. You deserve it."

I thought about Mum, and how I'd been so sad, for so long. How I'd lost touch with Marlon, too.

"I understand," I told her. "Goodbye."

She nuzzled my cheek before jumping into the jeep. There, she settled on her paws.

Randall came back, blinking with astonishment. "If it wasn't so weird," he said, "I'd swear you can talk to her." I grinned but said nothing.

"She will be safe," he said again.

"I know," I replied.

Faith and Marlon came and stood beside me. Faith took hold of my hand. When Randall drove away, I started to cry a little.

"Goodbye, friend," I whispered. "Goodbye, Mum – "

VERITY AND THE WOLF

curiosity

intrigue

discovery

protection

honesty

passion

trust

hope

79

Ideas for reading

Written by Gill Matthews
Primary Literacy Consultant

Reading objectives:

- check that the book makes sense, discussing their understanding and exploring the meaning of words in context
- draw inferences such as inferring characters' feelings, thoughts and motives from their actions, and justify inferences with evidence
- provide reasoned justification for views

Spoken language objectives:

- use relevant strategies to build their vocabulary
- articulate and justify answers, arguments and opinions
- use spoken language to develop understanding through speculating, hypothesising, imagining and exploring ideas

Curriculum links: Relationships Education – Families and people who care for me; Caring friendships

Interest words: curiosity, intrigue, discovery, protection, honesty, passion, trust, hope

Resources: ICT, paper and art materials

Build a context for reading

- Give children time to explore the cover of the book. Ask them to explain what they think the story is about.
- Read the blurb together. Focus on the phrase *no matter the cost …* Ask children what they think that means and why it ends with an ellipsis.
- Point out that this is a contemporary story. Ask children what they think that means.

Understand and apply reading strategies

- Read Chapter 1 aloud to the children. Check children's understanding by asking questions that require them to make inferences, for example *Who, or what, did Verity see in the woods? Why do you think she loved going to the woods?*
- Ask children to read Chapter 2 and then to briefly summarise it. Ask them why they think Verity calls the maple tree stump, *My tree stump?*